GORMAN

and the Treasure Chest

To the Monte Vista School,
Best Wishes!
John Steadman
1988

Bradbury Press   Scarsdale, New York

GORMAN
and the Treasure Chest

by John Stadler

Bradbury Press, Inc.
2 Overhill Road
Scarsdale, N.Y. 10583
An affiliate of Macmillan, Inc.
Collier Macmillan Canada, Inc.
Manufactured in the United States of America
2 4 6 8 10 9 7 5 3 1
The text of this book is set in 18 pt. Janson. The illustrations are full color pen and ink watercolor paintings, reproduced in halftone.
Library of Congress Cataloging in Publication Data
Stadler, John.
  Gorman and the treasure chest.
  Summary: When Gorman catches a chest instead of a fish in Treasure Lake, everyone is eager to help him open it and have for himself the treasure that must surely be inside.
  [1. Fishing—Fiction]   I. Title
PZ7.S77575Go   1984   [E]   82-9583
ISBN 0-02-786650-5

To Grandma Sid
and Grandma Doris
Grandpa Joe
and Grandpa Morris

Gorman was a locksmith. He made keys that always worked and locks that never broke, but best of all, he could open *anything*. If someone was locked out of a house, he could open the door. If someone couldn't open a bottle, Gorman would do it. Gorman was always busy, except on his day off. On that day Gorman went fishing on Treasure Lake.

"It's so relaxing," he said.

One day as Gorman floated on Treasure Lake,
something really big tugged on his line.

"Hot dog!" he squealed, "I've got a fish!"

But the fish had Gorman! It yanked him right
out of his boat and into the water, hauling him down
into the depths of Treasure Lake.

Struggling to get free, the huge fish dragged Gorman through the reeds at the bottom of the lake. Suddenly Gorman saw a large wooden chest hidden among the reeds. He immediately let go of the line.

"A treasure chest! I found the treasure chest! That's much better than a fish."

But a large turtle saw the treasure too. He dove into the reeds and pushed Gorman aside. The turtle swept the chest onto his back and headed for shore. Gorman grabbed the turtle's tail and held on.

"Come back with that," he gurgled.

On shore the turtle danced round and round in glee. "It's mine. It's my treasure chest," he shouted. "All for me, none for you. Go away!"

Catching his breath Gorman said, "It's mine too and anyway, that's a lock *you* could never open."

"Get lost!" snapped the turtle.

All their shouting attracted a huge bear who lumbered out of the forest. He spotted the treasure chest and without a word, hoisted it onto his shoulder and lumbered off with a big grin.

"You can't do that," shouted the stunned turtle, chasing after him. "Come back! Come back!"
The two disappeared into the forest.

"Run away all you like!" Gorman said shaking his head. "But that lock won't be easy pickings. It's been underwater a long, long time. It's probably rusted, jammed, broken and just plain ornery.

Gorman decided to go home.

"They'll need me, if they ever want to see what's inside that treasure chest," he said.

Suddenly Gorman heard the sound of many angry voices and fell to the ground. He crept forward and peeked over the plants.

There, in the clearing stood the bear and turtle, surrounded by a group of nasty looking creatures.

"I am Sir Diddily Whippet," growled a dog, "and these are my loyal scoundrels. I'll thank you to hand over that treasure . . . *now!*"

The scoundrels knocked the chest from the bear's shoulder.

They kicked it and clawed it. It didn't open, so they stabbed it and shot it. But the chest remained shut tight. Gorman stood up and shouted over the noise.

"That's no way to open that chest. Let me show you how it's done," he said. "Then we can all share whatever's inside."

"*Share?*" Sir Diddily groaned.

"Share *my* treasure," gasped the turtle, "No way!"

While the others argued and argued, the bear snatched up the chest and charged off again. Sir Diddily and the scoundrels pursued him, swords drawn, horns blaring. The turtle chased behind, screeching, "Mine! It's mine. Come back."

"There they go again," Gorman said. "When will they ever learn?"

It was getting late and Gorman headed home.

"Hot dog!" Gorman said when he reached his house. There waiting for him were Sir Diddily, the turtle, the bear, and all the scoundrels.

Sir Diddily ran up and hugged Gorman.

"I need you to open my treasure chest," he said.

"*OUR* treasure chest," said Gorman.

"Yes, I'll . . . I mean, *we'll* share it with you,"
the turtle hissed.

"Yeah!" grunted the bear.

Gorman went right to work as the others gathered around. They watched him closely.

Gorman worked quickly and before too long
there was a loud click. The lock was open!

"Mine! Mine! Mine!" the turtle shrieked.

The bear raised his two fists, Sir Diddily whipped
his sword high in the air. Gorman lifted the lid and
they all looked in. Nobody said a word!

A small creature climbed out of the chest and
dusted himself off. He looked around at everyone and
tipped his hat.

"Thank you. Thank you," he said, looking at his
watch. "I'd love to stay and chat, but I really must
be going."

The bear fell to his knees and howled at the moon. The turtle crawled inside his shell and refused to come out. And Sir Diddily fainted into the arms of his scoundrels who carried him off.

Meanwhile, Gorman dragged the empty chest into his workroom.

"That's quite a nice chest!" he said and went to bed.

Gorman continued to spend time at Treasure Lake. The years rolled by and Gorman grew older and less pink. Never again did he catch another fish. And that was just fine with him.